Seriously Silly Stories

FOOLISH JACK
and the
BEAN STACK

Compass Point Books
3109 West 50th Street, #115
Minneapolis, MN 55410

Visit Compass Point Books on the Internet at *www.compasspointbooks.com*
or e-mail your request to *custserv@compasspointbooks.com*

Library of Congress Cataloging-in-Publication Data
Anholt, Laurence.
   Foolish Jack and the bean stack / by Laurence Anholt. Illustrated by Arthur Robins.
     p. cm. — (Seriously silly stories)
Summary: In this humorous version of "Jack and the Beanstalk," Jack trades in the family cow for a can of beans.
ISBN 0-7565-0629-8 (hardcover)
   [1. Fairy tales. 2. Humorous stories.] I. Title II. Series: Anholt, Laurence. Seriously silly stories.
   PZ8.A577Fo 2004
   [E]—dc22   2003017950

For more information on *Foolish Jack,* use FactHound
to track down Web sites related to this book.

  1. Go to *www.compasspointbooks.com/facthound*
  2. Type in this book ID: 0756506298
  3. Click on the *Fetch It* button.

Your trusty FactHound will fetch the best Web sites for you!

About the Author
Laurence Anholt is one of the UK's leading authors. From his home in Dorset, he has produced more than 80 books, which are published all around the world. His Seriously Silly Stories have won numerous awards, including the Smarties Gold Award for "Snow White and the Seven Aliens."

About the Illustrator
Arthur Robins has illustrated more than 50 picture books, all of them highly successful and popular titles, and is the illustrator for all the Seriously Silly Stories. His energetic and fun-filled drawings have been featured in countless magazines, advertisements, and animations. He lives with his wife and two daughters in Surrey, England.

First published in Great Britain by Orchard Books, 96 Leonard Street, London EC2A 4XD

Text © Laurence Anholt 1996/Illustrations © Arthur Robins 1996

© 2004 by Compass Point Books

Printed in the United States of America.

Seriously Silly Stories

FOOLISH JACK
and the
BEAN STACK

Written by Laurence Anholt
Illustrated by Arthur Robins

COMPASS POINT BOOKS
Minneapolis, Minnesota

Foolish Jack and his mother were so poor...

...they lived under a cow in a field. His mom
slept at the front end...

...and Jack slept at the udder end.

Daisy was a good cow, but the problem was, Jack's mom was fed up with milk. It was all they ever had—
hot milk,
cold milk,
warm milk,
milk on toast,
milk cake.

And on Sundays, for a special treat, they had Milk Surprise (which was really just milk with milk on top).

Jack didn't mind milk, but his mother would have given anything for a change.

"I'M SICK AND TIRED OF MILK!" she would shout. "If I never taste another drop as long as I live, it will be too soon. If only you were a clever boy, Jack, you would think of something."

"I have thought of something," said Jack. "It's a new kind of milkshake—it's milk flavored."

Jack's mom chased him all around the field.

One day, a terrible thing happened. Jack was sitting in the field eating a Mini Milk lollipop and his mom was having her after-milk rest when Daisy suddenly looked up at the gray sky, decided it was going to rain, and, as all cows do, lay down.

13

"That is it! I've had enough!" spluttered Jack's mom when Jack had pulled her out by the ankles. "You will have to take Daisy into town and sell her. But make sure you get a good price, or I'll chase you around the field for a week."

Foolish Jack was very sad because Daisy was more like a friend than just a roof over his head. But he always liked to please his mother.

He made himself a milk sandwich for the journey, and Jack and Daisy set off toward the town. It was a long way, so they took turns carrying each other.

Then at the top of a hill, they met an
old man sitting on a tree stump with a
shopping bag.

"That's a fine cow you're carrying," he said. "What's your name, sonny?"

"It's Jack," said Jack, "but everyone calls me Foolish. I don't know why."

"Well, Jack," said the old man. "I'd like to buy that cow from you."

"I would like to sell this cow, too," said Jack, "but you'll have to give me a good price for her. Otherwise my mom will chase me around the field for a week."

"I can see you're a clever boy," said the old man, "and I'm in a good mood today. So guess what I'm going to give you for that cow?"

"What?" said Jack.

The old man reached into his shopping bag.

"Beans!" said the old man. "Not just one bean! Not just two beans! I'm going to give you A WHOLE CAN OF BAKED BEANS."

Jack couldn't believe his luck. Not one bean, not two beans, but a WHOLE CAN of baked beans for just one old cow. It must have been his lucky day. At last his mom would be proud of him.

So Jack kissed Daisy goodbye and set off
for home carrying the can of beans as care-
fully as he would carry a newborn baby,
feeling very pleased with himself.

23

As soon as he saw the field he began to shout, "Look Mom! All our troubles are over. Guess what I got for Daisy? Not one bean. Not two beans. But A WHOLE CAN COMPLETELY FULL OF BEANS! Why, mother there must be A HUNDRED yummy beans in this can. I knew you'd be pleased."

At the end of the week, when his mom had finished chasing him, Foolish Jack and his mom sat down in the middle of the field.

"Oh Jack," wailed his mom. "Now we haven't even got a cow to sleep under. If only you were a clever boy, you'd think of something."

"I have thought of something, mom," said Jack. "Let's eat the beans."

So Foolish Jack and his mom ate the beans. Then they had nothing left at all.

That night, Jack couldn't sleep. "I can't do anything right," he thought sadly. "My poor Mother would be better off without me. I think I will run away into the big wide world and seek my fortune."

So Jack decided to leave a note for his mother. He couldn't find any paper, so he tore the label from the bean can. But there was something already written on the back of the baked bean label.

Jack held the paper up to the moonlight and read aloud...

CONGRATULATIONS!
You have bought
THE LUCKY BEAN CAN
and won a
FANTASTIC PRIZE
for you and
your family!

Jack woke his mother. When she saw the message on the bean can, she couldn't believe her eyes. "Oh Jack!" she cried. "At last we will be able to buy a real house."

"Yes," said Jack, "and I will buy poor Daisy back. I would like a nice glass of milk."

And Jack's mom was too happy to chase him around the field.

In the morning they sent off the lucky bean label and soon their prize arrived—A WHOLE TRUCKLOAD OF BAKED BEANS.

Jack and his mom didn't know what to say.
They began to stack the cans in one corner of
the field, but before they had finished, a second
truckload of beans arrived.

And all day long the trucks kept coming.

By the evening there was a huge pile of bean cans. A STACK of bean cans. A COLOSSAL GLEAMING MONUMENTAL MOUNTAIN of bean cans. There were bean cans right up to the clouds.

So from that day Foolish Jack and his mom ate beans. It was all they ever had—

hot beans,
cold beans,
warm beans,
beans on toast,
bean cake.

And on Sundays, for a special treat, they had Bean Surprise (which was really just beans with beans on top).

Jack's mom would have given anything for a change.

"I'm SICK AND TIRED OF BEANS!" she shouted one day. "If I never eat another bean as long as I live, it will be too soon. If only you were a clever boy, Jack, you would think of something."

"I have thought of something," said Jack.
"Bean juice milkshake."

There wasn't room to chase Jack around the field because the bean stack was too big. So Jack's mom chased him up the bean stack instead.

Higher and higher, Jack hopped from can to can with his mom puffing and panting behind,

until at last Jack climbed so high he left his mom far behind. But Jack didn't stop. He kept on climbing. He looked down at the world below. He saw the field as small as a handkerchief and his mom as tiny as an ant. And still Jack climbed higher.

When he was almost too tired to climb any more, Jack reached the top of the bean stack, way up in the clouds.

Jack looked around. To his amazement he saw an enormous castle with its great door wide open.

He tiptoed inside. It was the most incredible place he had ever seen.

Jack wandered from room to room. He found massive bedrooms with carpets as thick as snowdrifts, a solar-heated Jacuzzi, a living room with great armchairs, and a TV screen the size of a cinema.

At last, Jack
wandered into a
wonderful kitchen
fitted with every
kind of gadget.

Jack was interested in cooking, and he climbed up to look at the giant-sized microwave.

Suddenly, the whole castle began to shake. A great voice roared.

Jack looked around in alarm and saw an enormous giant sitting at a table, rubbing his stomach and looking very miserable.

"It's not fair!" complained the giant. "All I ever get to eat is CHILDREN! And now I've got a bellyache..."

49

"Hot kids,
cold kids,
warm kids,
kids on toast,
kid cake.
And on Sundays,
for a special treat,
I have Kid Surprise
(but that's just kids
with kids on top).
I'd give ANYTHING for a change. I'M SICK
AND TIRED OF KIDS! If I never ate another
kid as long as I live it would be too soon..."
He looked down at Jack. "AND NOW I'VE
GOT TO EAT YOU, TOO! IT'S NOT FAIR!"

The giant reached out a huge hairy hand and grabbed Jack around the waist.

He lifted Jack kicking and struggling into the air and opened his vast black cavelike mouth with a tongue like a huge purple carpet.

"Well," thought Jack, "this is the end of Foolish Jack, no doubt."

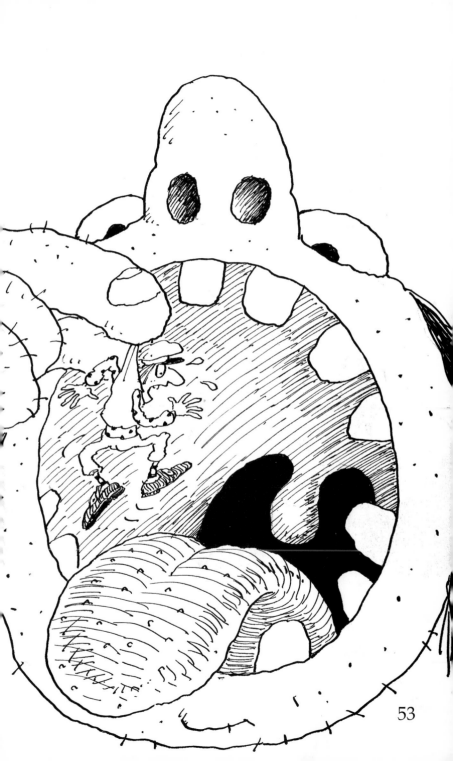

He was just about to be crunched into a million tiny foolish pieces, when suddenly he had an idea.

"Er, excuse me, Mr. Giant," he whispered nervously. "If you eat me it will only make your tummyache worse. I can think of something much nicer. I don't suppose you like... beans do you?"

"BEANS!" roared the giant "DO I LIKE BEANS? I YUMMY YUMMY LOVE 'em!"

So Jack took the giant by the hand and led him down the bean stack. And on the way, the giant told Jack how lonely he was, all by himself in the great big castle in the clouds with nothing to do but eat people.

Jack began to feel very sorry for the poor
giant and took him home to meet his mom.

"Oh Jack," she cried. "Where ever have you bean?"

Jack's mom was very pleased to see Jack in one piece. But when she saw the giant...!

And when the giant saw Jack's mom...!

It was love at first sight.

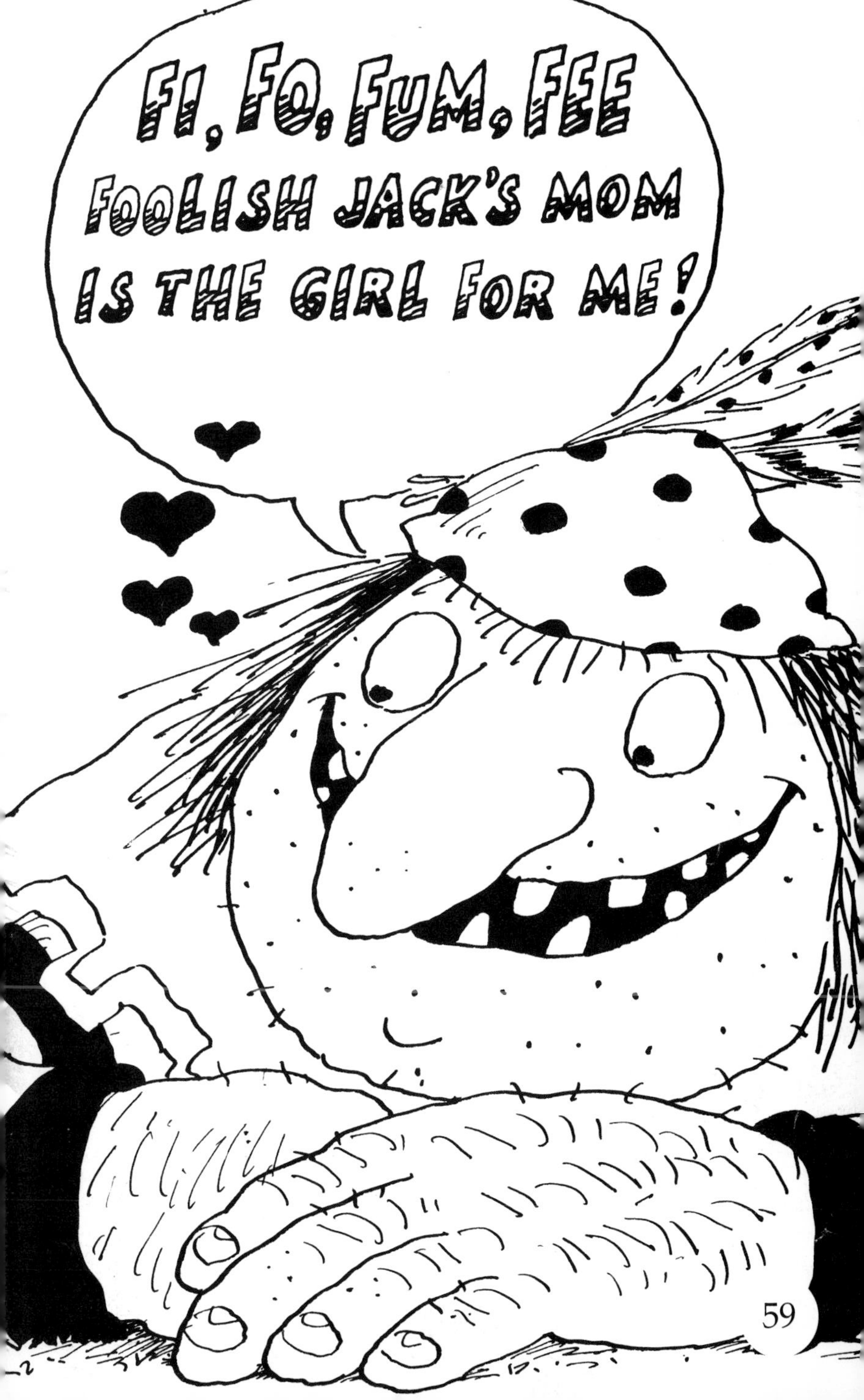
FI, FO, FUM, FEE
FOOLISH JACK'S MOM
IS THE GIRL FOR ME!

"Of course I am, dear," said Jack's mom, "but first you must be hungry after your long journey."

The giant looked at the bean stack, gleaming in the evening light as he licked his giant lips.

He began munching the beans. Not one can, not two cans, but the whole stack of beans. And he didn't even stop to open the cans.

So Foolish Jack's mom married the giant, and they were very happy. They all went to live in the giant's wonderful castle in the sky.

Foolish Jack opened a cafe in the giant's kitchen and he called it FOOLISH JACK'S SKY SNACKS. And people came from far and wide and Jack grew rich and happy.

He served everything you can think of except milk...

and beans!